MW00999405

Climb up the wistful, mistful hill
where weeping gargoyles sit.
Slip past the gloomful, moonful graves
where small ghosts peer and flit.

Walk up the weary, dreary path
where scarab beetles crawl.
Come in the sneaky, creaky door
and pace the doom-dark hall.

Twilight's here.
The death bell rings.
Everyone knows what
the death bell brings . . .

It's time for class. You're in the place
where goblins wail and zombies drool.
(That's because they're kindergartners.)
Welcome to . . .

MONSTER SCHOOL

By **Kate Coombs**

Pictures by **Lee Gatlin**

chronicle books · san francisco

Stevie the Loser

Stevie always loses things.
Today he lost his arm.
He lost his mittens yesterday
and his anti-lose-things charm.

Stevie lost his kneecap.
Stevie lost his nose.
He lost his homework, lost his snack,
and now he's lost his toes.

"Come on," calls Mrs. Appleby.
"Everyone help look!"
Now Stevie's lost an eyeball
and his backpack and a book.

The backpack's in the corner.
The book's beneath a desk.
We find the homework and the toes
but give up on the rest.

Monster Mash

Me? I'm multicultural. I come from here and there.
That's why I have a bunch of claws and floating purple hair.

Great-grandma Exomandras had a wand for zapping things.
Great-grandpa Fog had seven horns and two enormous wings.

Great-grandma Jane liked bridges, and her favorite meal was goat.
She met Great-grandpa Anton in a deep and slithery moat.

Great-grandma Rose was elven, and she always dressed in green.
Great-grandpa George was boggart and was just a little mean.

The last of my great-grandmas built her houses out of cake.
The last of my great-grandpas often turned into a snake.

And now I'm me, but as you see,
I come from everyplace.
That's why I have
three scaly tails
and move with fairy grace.

I'm really multicultural.
Are you multicultural too?
I see a lot of things now that
I take a look at you.

My Family Tree

Song of the Freckles

You hear her voice before you see her
coming down the hall toward you.
Her voice has lots of smiles in it
and makes you smile too.

She keeps her magic in her freckles—
that's what people say.
I just know she really sees me,
asking, "How are you today?"

She likes it when you tell her jokes.
Then she tells some and laughs a lot.
She waves at someone, drops her books,
and shows you beetles that she caught.

Spiders ride her shoulders,
her clothes are trimmed in spider lace.
Ants crawl up and down her arms,
she has twelve freckles on her face.

Off she goes, she's always singing,
old songs, new songs, songs she makes—
they'll get you dreaming sunny mornings,
your favorite tree, and chocolate cakes.

She isn't someone on TV,
but we all listen when she speaks.
Her spells are made of spiderwebs
and those twelve freckles on her cheeks.

Gargoyle

I'm alone in my stone.
Always frowning
like I just got some bad news.
Wings always lifting
as if I really could fly.

I am gray and marked
by lichen on one side.
Gargoyle, they call me,
just gargoyle.
But I know my name.

It's Nice

It's nice to be shy. People say it's not,
but they don't know. Sometimes I like to watch
the other kids playing. Other times I look
at the trees, the way a branch sways a little
when a bird lands on it. During recess,
I take my book outside and sit on the steps.

People call me a ghost, like my edges are fluttering.
But I'm just quiet, the way a night
shines with stars that aren't saying a word.

Fernanda Kabul

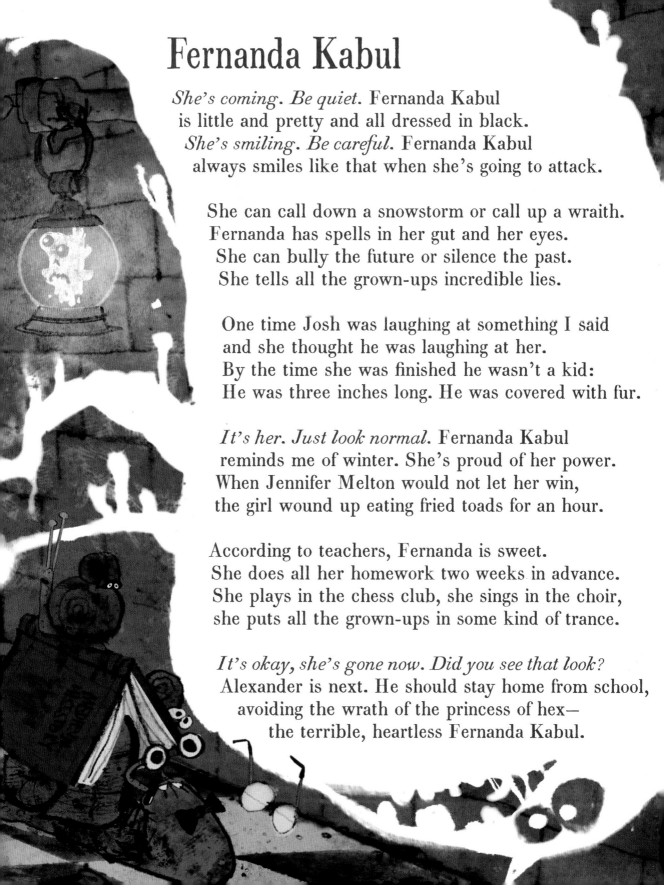

She's coming. Be quiet. Fernanda Kabul
is little and pretty and all dressed in black.
She's smiling. Be careful. Fernanda Kabul
always smiles like that when she's going to attack.

She can call down a snowstorm or call up a wraith.
Fernanda has spells in her gut and her eyes.
She can bully the future or silence the past.
She tells all the grown-ups incredible lies.

One time Josh was laughing at something I said
and she thought he was laughing at her.
By the time she was finished he wasn't a kid:
He was three inches long. He was covered with fur.

It's her. Just look normal. Fernanda Kabul
reminds me of winter. She's proud of her power.
When Jennifer Melton would not let her win,
the girl wound up eating fried toads for an hour.

According to teachers, Fernanda is sweet.
She does all her homework two weeks in advance.
She plays in the chess club, she sings in the choir,
she puts all the grown-ups in some kind of trance.

It's okay, she's gone now. Did you see that look?
Alexander is next. He should stay home from school,
avoiding the wrath of the princess of hex—
the terrible, heartless Fernanda Kabul.

Graveyard Ball

Okay. Home plate is Agnes Crump,
first base is Frederick Howl.
Second is Camphor Medley
and third is Prudence Powell.
Swing the bone bat at the skull,
then run around the bases.
Do not trip over any graves
or knock down funeral vases.
Don't let the ghouls grab you
or you won't make it home.
We'll try to get you back before
you're in the catacomb.

Don't argue with Coach Gorey—
he's much worse than he seems.
You don't want to know what happens
if he cuts you from the team.

Cafeteria Food

Everything tastes pretty good:
cricket quiche and french-fried brain,
old shoe stew and ankle cake,
  spider biscuits, auk chow mein.

  Monday's always frog surprise.
    Tuesday's dragon wings on toast.
    Wednesday's alligator soup—
      but we like Friday food the most.

    Thursday we eat toadstool buns
  or cookies made from glue.
    But Friday's what we're waiting for—
  we'll save a slice for you.

  Oh, pickled
    donkey tails
    are nice,
    and
    curried
  earthworm
    tea.
  But we
    can't wait
    till Friday night—
      come eat with us
      and see!

Homework

Homework, stupid homework:
I'm supposed to catch a newt
and write a three-page essay
on the Dragon Institute.

Homework, dumb old homework:
I've got to make a graph
about the history of witches
and write an epitaph.

Homework, boring homework:
I have to create a curse,
then make a model skeleton
and write a ten-line verse.

I ought to do my homework:
Instead I watch TV
and play eight games of Vampire World
and snooze repeatedly.

My teacher's going to kill me:
Last time that's what she said.
But I'm just not that worried
because I'm already dead.

I Am Glorious

I am glorious, I am royal.
You may not speak to me.
I am a child of the ancient Nile,
second cousin to Nefertiti.

All of you really should bow down
whenever you look my way.
I must not rumple my wrappings.
Of course I don't want to play.

I am wearing golden slippers,
just in case you cannot tell.
I am dressed in pure white linen
and adorned with jewels as well.

*Oh, to be a child of the
ancient Nile is a fine and
prideful thing.
But I wish a little,
sometimes, I could talk
to people or swing.*

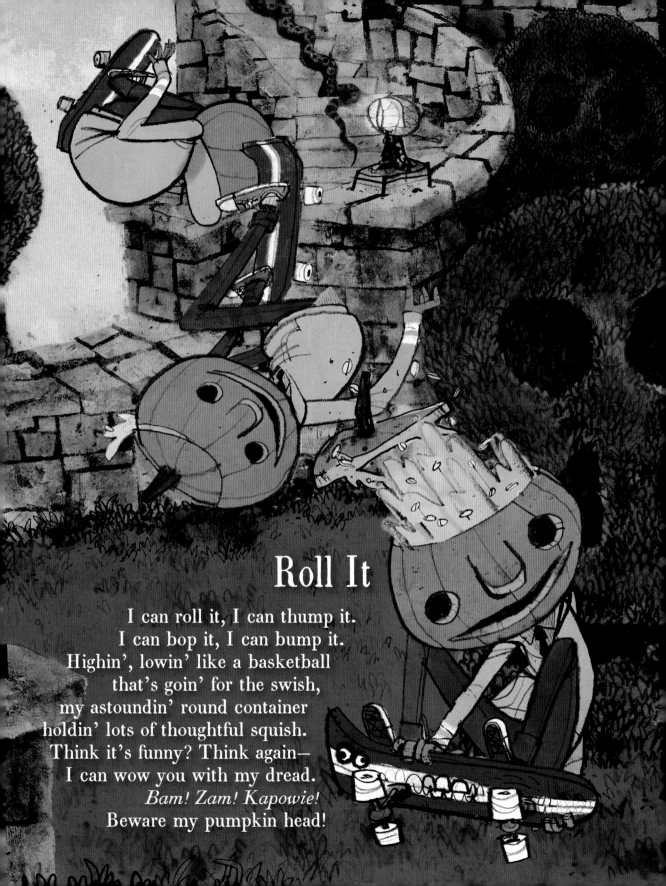

Roll It

I can roll it, I can thump it.
I can bop it, I can bump it.
Highin', lowin' like a basketball
    that's goin' for the swish,
my astoundin' round container
holdin' lots of thoughtful squish.
Think it's funny? Think again—
I can wow you with my dread.
    Bam! Zam! Kapowie!
Beware my pumpkin head!

Computer Wizard

I've written a program for baffling parents
and one for confounding my teachers.
I've created an app that becomes a net
to capture odd magical creatures.

I can make myself sit in assembly and smile
when I'm really a light year away.
My programs can paint like Picasso, can burp,
and can turn a whole neighborhood gray.

My mouse feeds on virtual crackers and cheese.
My ram feeds on virtual grass.
I can conquer the Web with my virtual spiders
while I'm doing my homework for class.

I have WizPads and voiceprints and devious games,
hacking skills I have not even used.
With my tech I can do almost anything, but
word problems still leave me confused.

Hair Care

Everyone asks to braid my hair,
but the snakes just don't like it.
Girls bring their combs and their gel—
they think they can spike it.

But snakes hate sticking up.
They'd rather twist and twirl.
If you want to fix my hair,
you have to go for curl.

No curling irons, though.
It's more like training them.
They curl well if you're nice
and softly stroke their skin.

The mambas are Freddy and Eddy.
The kraits are Jess and Sue.
The adders on top are Basilia
and Coil and Melissa and Boo.

Around the back I've got cobras—
Yuri and Madeline.
The vipers are Max and Athena,
Slink, Lara, and Caroline.

I know, they're all venomous snakes.
I have extra special hair.
Their fangs can be kind of deadly,
but not as bad as their stare.

In first grade I knew this girl
who wouldn't leave me alone.
I told her don't yank, please be gentle,
but she got turned to stone.

So yeah, you can fix my hair—
no braids, no pulling, no heat.
Ask them to help you out
and my snakes are pretty sweet.

Science Fair Sonnet

So every year we have a science fair.
I need a new experiment. A plan.
Last year I studied how to grow more hair.
My little sister looked just like a man.

This time I want to know how griffins fly—
their wingspan doesn't seem to hold their weight.
Another thing I want to know is why
a dead eel is so hard to animate.

Of course the other kids are going to whine.
I'm not sure what they're always fussing for.
I can't help that my grandpa's Frankenstein
or that I have my very own Igor.

They say I'm bad with nitroglycerin,
but they're just jealous that I'm going to win.

Compare and Contrast

Ms. Blackhurst is a banshee.
She has burning eyes.
She gets mad a lot.
When she does, she screams
like horrible dreams
in a voice that's filled with rot.

Ms. Raju is a nagi.
She hisses and weaves when she speaks.
Her whispering slithers
like fog and it withers
whatever it touches for weeks.

Which is worse, the hiss or the yell?
It's not that we aren't brave.
But each one's tough.
It's almost enough
to make us sit up and behave.

Ghost Girl's Lament

Haunting people is an art.
A proud one, my grandpa always said.
You don't just fly shrieking down the hall.
You whisper. Then leave an eerie silence.
You wind like fog around the chandelier
or glimmer up and down the staircase.

But this place? I just can't.
It's unbearable. Little goblins
howling in the cafeteria, and the stomping
every day when school gets out!

I shiver through the science lab,
but that kid Matthew tells me go away.
Go away? So instead I hide
in the coat closet and when someone comes
to get their coat I moan, nice and gloomy.
"Hi, Ghost!" says whoever it is,
and I see she's a tall purple monster—
so what does she care about ghosts?

The witch is the worst.
She doesn't even flinch. She just says,
"Stay out of my way, Sophie,
or I'll turn you to lint." How
does she know my name? Then I try
haunting the teachers, but it's no use.
"Young lady," Mr. Crow says,
"why don't you spend your time
in the library rather than my classroom?"

I go back to the coat closet. Groaning,
sighing, not because I'm haunting anyone.
No, I'm in here crying. *Boo-hoo.*

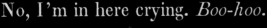

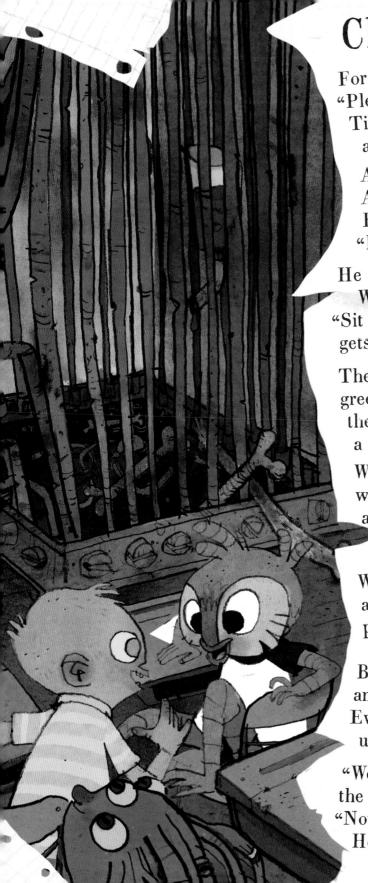

Class Pet

For weeks and weeks we begged him,
"Please, we have to have a pet!"
  Till he said yes, so then we talked
    about what kind to get.

  A chupacabra or an owl?
  A dire three-headed hound?
  But Mr. Winter shook his head.
"I'm going to the pound."

He did. He brought a covered cage.
  We crowded close to see.
"Sit down," he said. "Poor little thing
gets scared so easily."

The first we saw were yellow eyes,
green ears, a little maw,
  then six serrated feet. We took
  a vote and named him Claw.

  We learned to care for our new pet—
  we fed him moldy hay
    and mossy stones and grimy bones.
        He grew more every day.

  We had to get a bigger cage
  and buy a ton of food,
    plus leather gloves for petting Claw
    when he was in a mood.

  But then we got to school last week
  and found our pet was gone.
  Everyone was really sad—
    until the news came on.

"We've lost a postman and his truck,"
the news announcer said.
"Now something's eaten Mayor Grant."
  Hooray! Our pet's not dead!

New Kid

I'm Mr. Ordinary.
I earn my C's and B's.
Mr. Ordinary—
I run and I climb trees.

I mostly do my homework.
But other kids still sneer
in fakey not-quite whispers,
"So what's he doing here?"

I'm Mr. Ordinary.
I wear t-shirts and jeans.
Mr. Ordinary—
I do not eat string beans.

I love to run the bases.
I can pitch a winning game.
But people roll their eyes
whenever teachers say my name.

Sometimes kids try to scare me
with a spider or a skull.
Yeah, they'll think I'm ordinary . . .

. . . until the moon is full.

For my sister Holly —K. C.

For Amos —L. G.

Library of Congress Cataloging-in-Publication Data:
Names: Coombs, Kate, author. | Gatlin, Lee, illustrator.
Title: Monster school / by Kate Coombs ; illustrated by Lee Gatlin.
Description: San Francisco : Chronicle Books, 2018.
Identifiers: LCCN 2016030456 | ISBN 9781452129389 (alk. paper)
Subjects: LCSH: Monsters—Juvenile poetry.
Classification: LCC PS3603.O5796 A6 2017 | DDC 811/.6—dc23 LC record
available at https://lccn.loc.gov/2016030456

Manufactured in China.

MIX
Paper from
responsible sources
FSC™ C104723

Design by Amelia Mack.
Typeset in 1820 Modern.
The illustrations in this book were rendered in traditional and digital media.

10 9 8 7 6 5 4 3 2 1

Chronicle Books LLC
680 Second Street
San Francisco, California 94107

Chronicle Books—we see things differently.
Become part of our community at www.chroniclekids.com.